I Wear Long Green Hair in the Summer

P9-DCJ-700

I WEAR LONG GREEN HAIR IN THE SUMMER

Charlotte Agell

Tilbury House, Publishers
Gardiner, Maine

To my husband, Peter,
and to my father, Christer

Tilbury House, Publishers
132 Water Street
Gardiner, ME 04345

Text and Illustrations Copyright © 1994 by Charlotte Agell.

All Rights Reserved. No part of this publication may be reproduced or transmitted in any form or by any means, electronic or mechanical, including photocopy, recording or any information storage or retrieval system, without permission in writing from the publisher.

First Printing

Library of Congress Cataloging-in-Publications Data
Agell, Charlotte.
    I wear long green hair in the Summer / Charlotte Agell.
        p. cm.
    Summary: A young girl goes to the beach with her father and spends a long summer day playing in the waves, the sand, and the seaweed.
    ISBN 0-88448-113-1 : $7.95
    [1. Beaches--Fiction. 2. Summer--Fiction. 3. Fathers and daughters-- Fiction.] I. Title.
PZ7. A2665Iam   1994
[E]--dc20
                                                                                            93-33612
                                                                                            CIP
                                                                                            AC

Designed by Edith Allard and Charlotte Agell
Editing and production: Mark Melnicove, Lisa Reece,
Devon Phillips, and Lisa Holbrook
Office and warehouse: Jolene and Andrea Collins

Imagesetting: High Resolution, Inc., Camden, Maine
Color separations: Graphic Color Service, Fairfield, Maine
Printing: Eusey Press, Leominster, Massachusetts
Binding: The Book Press, Brattleboro, Vermont

It is too hot to sleep
and we all get up early.

Mama says the baby
has been up all night.
Maybe he's teething.

Papa and I are going to the beach,
so mama can rest.
Yippee! I pack all my toys.

We wave good-bye.
Mama looks a little grumpy
even though she smiles.

The car ride is long and hot.
The road is too twisty and I feel
a little carsick. But I don't throw up.

At last we are at the beach —
I can hear the waves crashing!

The sand on the path is too hot!
It burns my feet.
It makes me yell!

Super Papa picks me up.

We run to the cool sand by the water
with all the bugs chasing us.
Go away, bugs!

We put all our stuff on the blanket
so it won't blow away.
Then I put on my suit.

My brother would try to eat all this sand.

My papa says,
"The water is freezing."

I don't think so.
I play in the waves
a long, long time.

Here's a tidal pool
where the sun has warmed the water.

Papa lies down in the pool.
He is a CROCODILE.

I run away laughing —
and look! The gulls want our food.
They can open bags with their beaks.

Shoo, gulls, that's our picnic!

We have peanut butter and jam
and sand sandwiches. I throw
the crusts to the gulls,

but papa says,
"Don't encourage them!"
His newspaper flaps in the wind.

I find blue clay
under the sand, under the rocks.
I can make blue clay legs.

I wear long green hair
in the summer!
Seaweed hair, all wet and slapping.

Papa opens his eyes and says,
"Hello, Sea Creature!"

He says my lips are purple from the cold
water, and that it is time to go.
I say they are purple from blueberry jam.

I jump in the water
to wash off the clay.
The waves are full of children!

I don't want to go.
I just want to PLAY.

Papa sings a silly song
all the way home.

I smell like sunscreen
and I taste like salt.
My eyes don't want to stay open.

Mama and my brother
meet us at the door.
They are both smiling.

"We slept all day
and it was just what we needed,"
says mama.

I didn't sleep all day.
I went to the beach
with my papa.

Other books in this series by Charlotte Agell

MUD MAKES ME DANCE IN THE SPRING
WIND SPINS ME AROUND IN THE FALL
I SLIDE INTO THE WHITE OF WINTER

For more information write or call:
Tilbury House, Publishers
132 Water Street Gardiner, ME 04345
1-800-582-1899 Fax 207-582-8227